O is for Oklahoma

written by kids
for kids

WESTWINDS
PRESS®

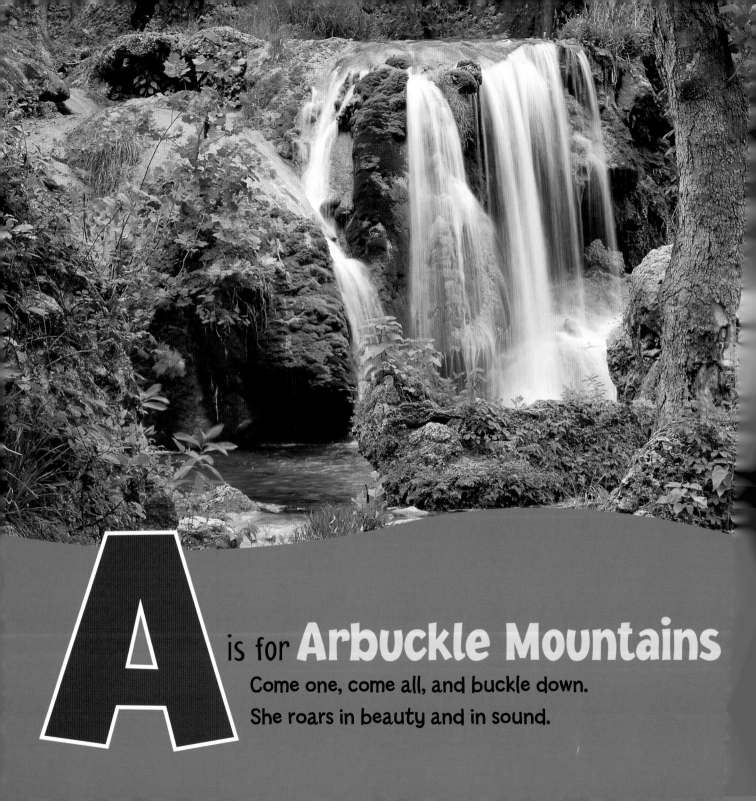

A is for **Arbuckle Mountains**

Come one, come all, and buckle down.
She roars in beauty and in sound.

B is for **Bison**

Millions of bison roamed these places,
With thick brown fur framing their faces.

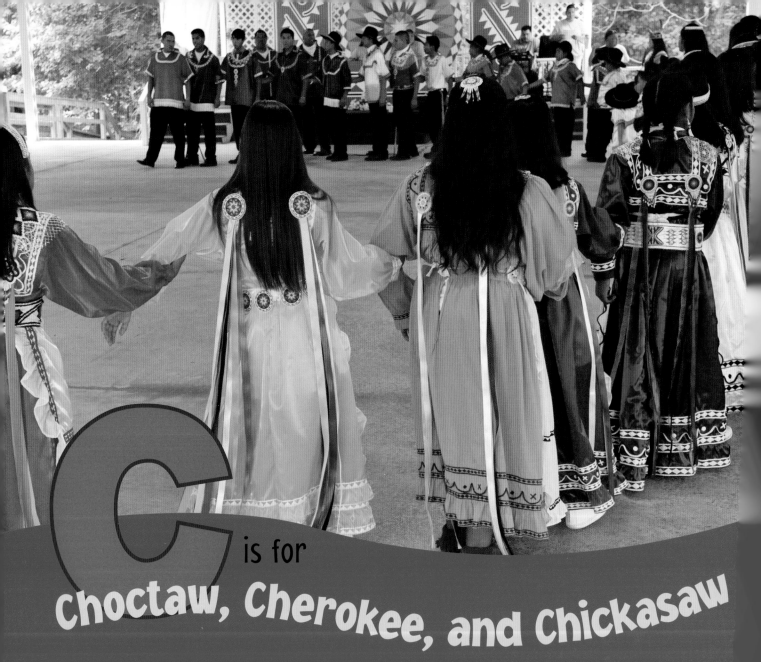

C is for

Choctaw, Cherokee, and Chickasaw

Knowing plants, animals, and the way of the land,
Native tribes sowed their wisdom and still they stand.

*Author's note: "I am a Native American in this tribe!"

D is for **Dust Bowl**

It stole ten of Oklahoma's years—
Dust blowing everywhere, up to your ears!

E

is for

Eufaula Lake

When I fish, I bring my pole
To our state's largest fishing hole.

F is for **Farms**

On a farm I see cute baby chicks.
And sometimes, fresh green peas I can pick!

G is for Great Salt Plains

The salt crystals were found long ago,
And the sand there, it looks just like snow.

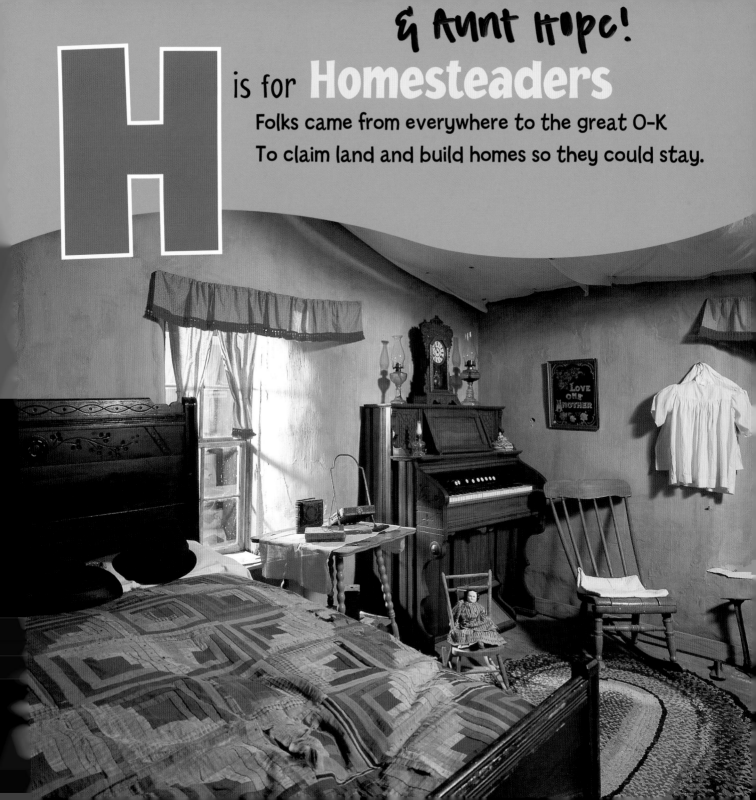

H

& Aunt Hope!

is for **Homesteaders**

Folks came from everywhere to the great O-K
To claim land and build homes so they could stay.

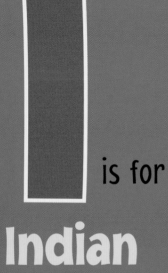 **is for**

Indian Blanket

Our state wildflower is
definitely not plain—
Its colors remind me of
a lion's mane.

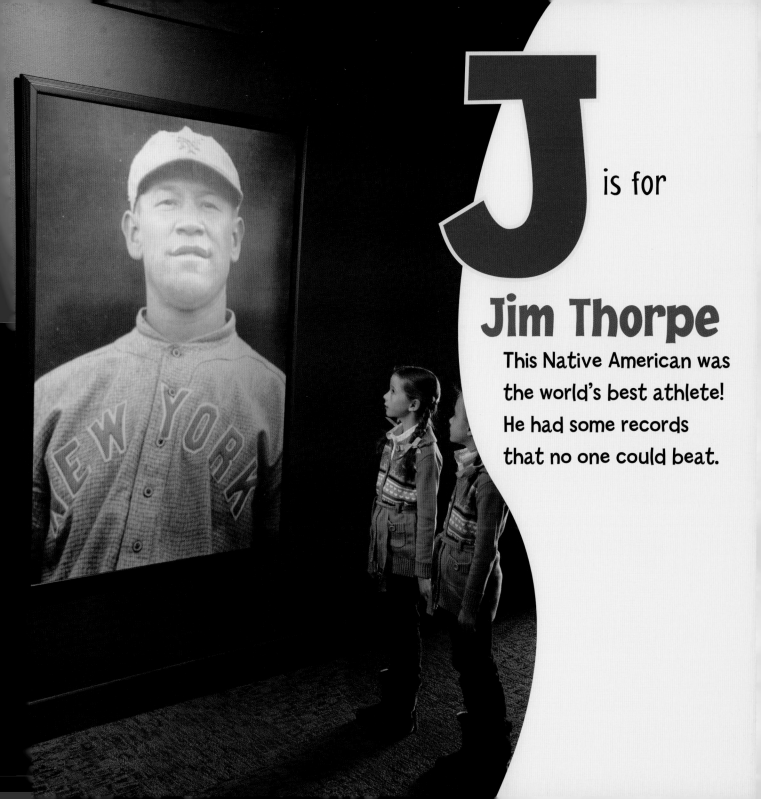

J is for

Jim Thorpe

This Native American was the world's best athlete! He had some records that no one could beat.

WHITE ONLY   COLORED ONLY

K

is for **Katz Drug Store**

At the first sit-in people had to be brave,
As they fought for the equality that they craved.

L

is for **Library**

Reading is power, we learn through and through.

I love to read, how about you?

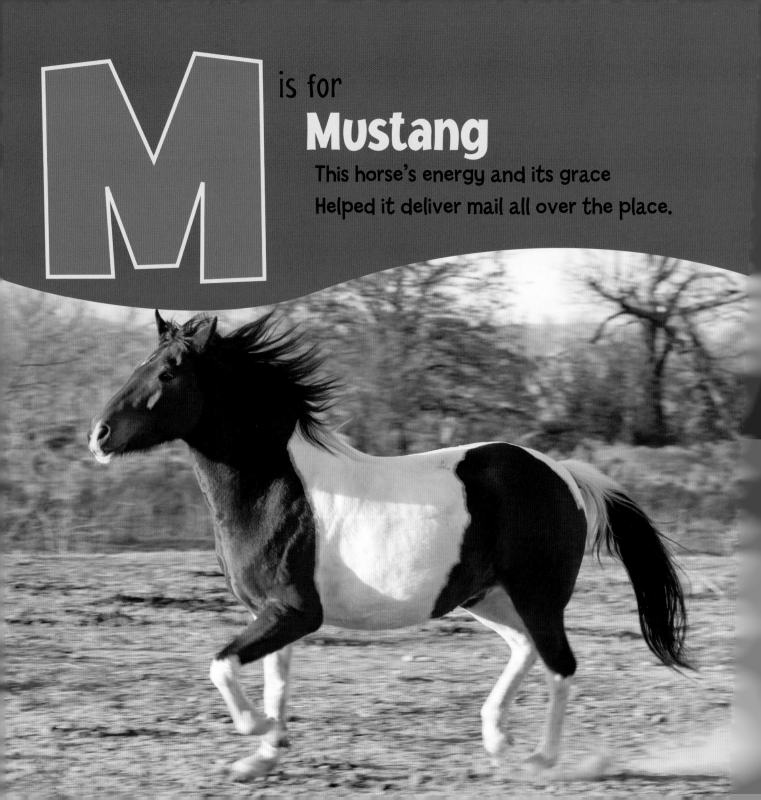

M is for **Mustang**

This horse's energy and its grace
Helped it deliver mail all over the place.

N is for natural Gas

We use natural gas to run cars and trucks,
And it doesn't cost a lot of bucks.

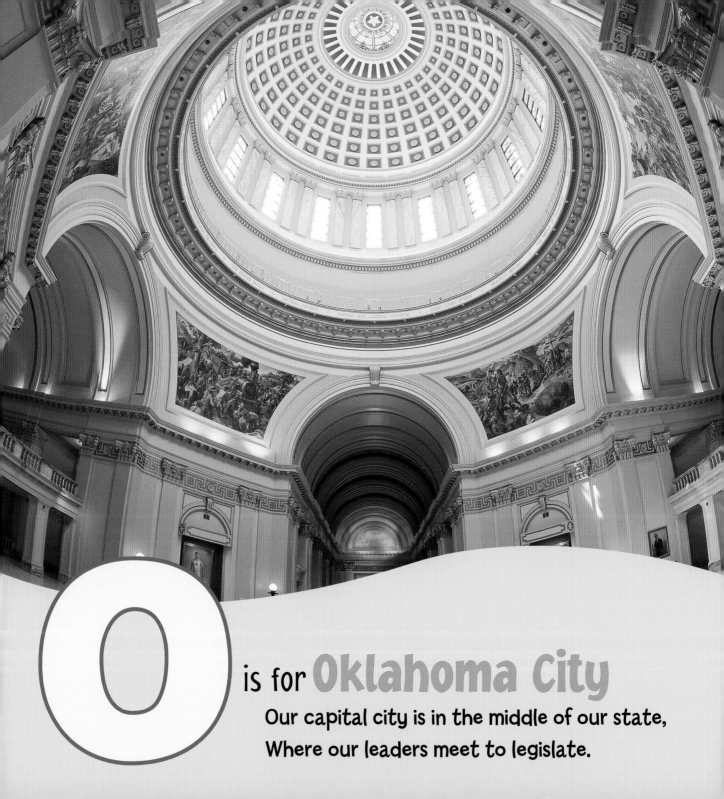

O

is for Oklahoma City

Our capital city is in the middle of our state,
Where our leaders meet to legislate.

P is for **Prairie**

The grass is so tall it touches the sky.
Here buffalo roam and eagles fly.

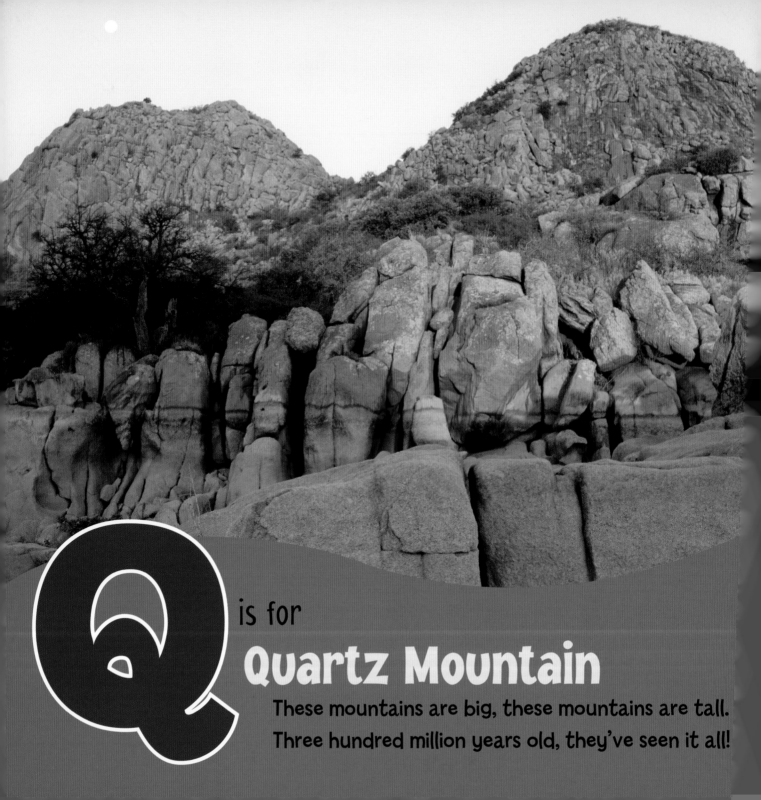

Q is for
Quartz Mountain

These mountains are big, these mountains are tall.
Three hundred million years old, they've seen it all!

R is for
Redbud Tree

The leaves on this tree look just like hearts.
When it blooms, you know spring's going to start.

S is for Scissor-Tailed Flycatcher

Our state bird is bold and fast.
You can hardly see him as he zooms past.

T

is for **Tulsa** & uncle Taylor !

Tulsa is our second-largest city.

Its green grassy hills make it very pretty.

U is for Underground

Underground

For a quick way to get around downtown
Why not head to the Underground?

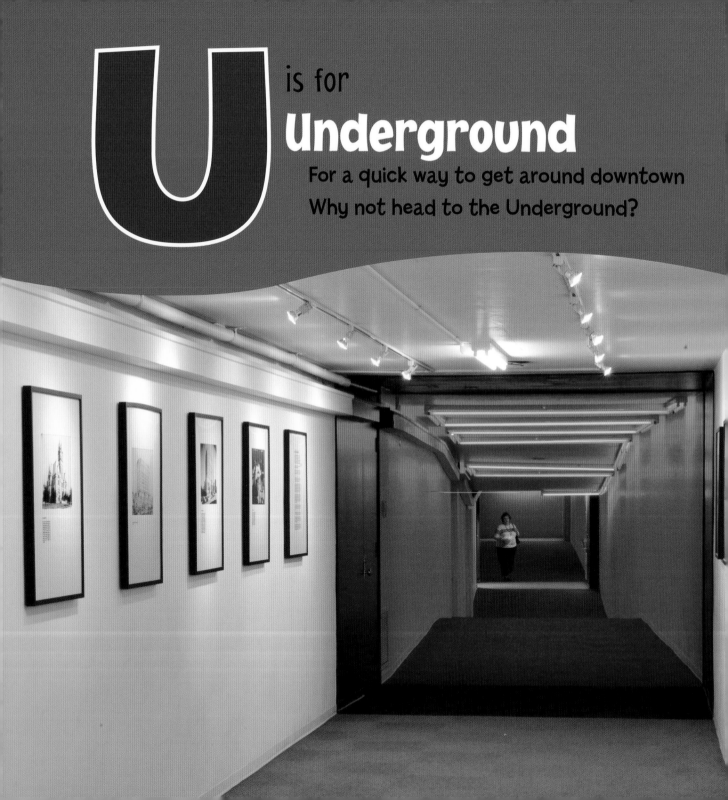

V is for **Vortex**

Beware our tornadoes, some of the fastest around!
The vortex whirls as it touches the ground.

W is for

Will Rogers

This cowboy performer was known for his humor. His honest wit made him a world-famous Sooner.

X is for eXtreme Weather

We get booming lightning
and crackling ice,
But the days we have
sunshine are really nice.

Y is for **Yvonne Chouteau**

A beautiful dancer, she leaped and twirled
Into hearts all over the world!

Z is for Zoo

Come see monkeys, giraffes, and a crocodile.
The baby elephant will make you smile!

Holy Smoke!

Arbuckle Mountains

These mountains are ancient—the granite is 1.4 billion years old! They were named for General Matthew Arbuckle, who established a post (later a fort) along Wildhorse Creek. Turner Falls, Price Falls, and the Chickasaw National Recreation Area are popular recreation spots.

Bison (also called "buffalo")

There were once tens of millions of bison, the state animal of Oklahoma, roaming our country. Their grazing and trampling behaviors helped shape the unique ecosystem of the Great Plains. But these magnificent animals came close to extinction in the 1800s due to overhunting. There are now about 300,000 bison left in North America. In Oklahoma you can find large herds thriving at the Wichita Mountains Wildlife Refuge and the Tallgrass Prairie Preserve.

Choctaw, Cherokee, and Chickasaw

Oklahoma has the second-largest Native American population of any state: more than a quarter of a million people! In the 1800s, white settlers and the government forcibly removed the tribes from their traditional lands to Oklahoma, then called "Indian Territory." Today there are dozens of tribes represented, including Apache, Cheyenne, Kiowa, Modoc, Osage, Pawnee, and Seminole.

Dust Bowl

With the invention of mechanized farm equipment in the early 1900s, the Oklahoma landscape changed dramatically. Farmers plowed under deep-rooted grasses that had previously kept soil and moisture in place during droughts. Bad idea! During the drought of the 1930s, without the native grass to keep soil in place, it dried, turned to dust, and blew away. Humungous dust storms erupted and clouds blackened the skies for days, reducing visibility to a few feet, and sometimes drifting as far away as New York City! Millions of acres of farmland were destroyed and hundreds of thousands of people, nicknamed "Okies," had to abandon their homes in search of a new life.

Eufaula Lake

This reservoir is the largest lake in Oklahoma. The dam that created it took eight years to build and provides hydroelectric power, while the lake provides a place for boating, swimming, hiking, and camping. Fishing is also a popular activity, since the lake is chock-full of bass, crappie, catfish, and stripers.

Farms

Oklahoma is farm country. The state is the #5 beef producer in the United States, and farmers also raise pigs, chickens, sheep, turkeys, and even catfish! The top crops are wheat, hay, cotton, soybeans, corn, pecans, peanuts, and watermelons. That's a lot of tasty food!

Great Salt Plains

This flat, barren, 11,000-acre marvel is named for the thin layer of salt that covers the area. The salt was deposited millions of years ago when a shallow sea covered this part of Oklahoma. Imagine—an ocean in the middle of America! Today visitors like to search for selenite crystals, which have a cool hourglass shape inside them.

Homesteaders

In 1862, President Lincoln signed the Homestead Act, which promised 160 acres of land in "unsettled" territories (including Oklahoma) to anyone who would build a home and farm on it. The rush of white settlers, called homesteaders, further displaced thousands of Native Americans who were already living there. Since there were few trees on the Great Plains, homesteaders there usually built their houses out of sod (bricks cut from the dirt, with grass roots still intact). Imagine keeping your room clean in a house made of dirt! Thousands of "soddies" once covered the Oklahoma prairies, but only one is left: the sod house built by Marshal McCully in 1894.

Facts about the

Indian Blanket

This bright, hardy flower grows in most kinds of soil and has a high tolerance for heat and drought. Perfect for Oklahoma! Also called firewheel, the Indian blanket flower is a symbol of the state's Native American history.

Jim Thorpe

A Sac and Fox Indian who grew up in Oklahoma, Thorpe's Indian name was Wa-Tho-Huk or "Bright Path," which described his future well. Thorpe was an amazing athlete who excelled in many sports. In 1912 he won Olympic gold medals in the pentathlon and decathlon, setting world records. Later he played professional football, baseball, and basketball! ABC Sports named him "Athlete of the Century," beating Muhammad Ali, Babe Ruth, and Michael Jordan!

Katz Drug Store

Prior to the 1950s, in many parts of America, businesses and restaurants were segregated—they refused to serve African Americans at the same tables and counters as white customers, or refused to serve them at all. During the civil rights movement, people fought to change that. In Oklahoma City in 1958, Clara Luper, an African-American high school teacher, along with her eight-year-old daughter and other students, led one of the nation's first "sit-ins." The protesters sat at the Katz Drug Store counter and refused to leave until they were served. It worked. Over the next few years, the protesters forced all Oklahoma restaurants to serve everyone.

Library

Oklahoma loves its libraries! There are 1.9 million Oklahomans with library cards and they check out 22 million books every year! State libraries also employ 1,893 Oklahomans. The dinosaur in the picture stands outside the Northwest Library in Oklahoma City. This seven-foot-tall saurophaganax in tennis shoes was designed by artist Solomon Bassoff.

Mustang

The ancestors of today's Mustangs first came to America with Spanish explorers. Some escaped or were captured by Native Americans, and quickly spread west. These horses changed the lives of the Native Americans living in the Great Plains, helping them travel farther and faster, and hunt more easily. Today there are about 30,000 wild mustangs roaming free in America, many in Oklahoma.

Natural Gas

Natural gas is one of the most popular forms of energy today. It is used to power everything from stoves to houses to garbage trucks! Natural gas is found all over Oklahoma—3,400 gas fields in all—and is one of the most important industries in the state.

Oklahoma City

Oklahoma City is the state capital and largest city in the state. It was founded during the Land Run of 1889, when thousands of homesteaders raced to claim town lots around Oklahoma Station. Within hours, this tiny railroad stop grew to a population of 10,000! And it kept growing. The metro area is now home to more than a million citizens. The Capitol Building was constructed in 1917 and, to save money, it originally had no dome. The gorgeous dome pictured is new, added to the Capitol in 2002.

Prairie

Most of Oklahoma is a prairie ecosystem, home to 650 different kinds of grasses, shrubs, and flowers, but very few trees. "Prairie" is the French word for "meadow," and indeed, remaining prairies are covered in meadow wildflowers like prairie iris, white wind flower, and blazing star. Animals like the prairie, too. If you're quiet, you might see some greater prairie chickens, a swift fox, and, of course, plenty of squeaking prairie dogs.

Quartz Mountain

Located in the southwestern corner of the state, this mountain is mostly pink-red Lugert granite, but you'll find plenty of quartz in there, too. Baldy Point is a popular rock-climbing destination, but there's also loads of camping, hiking, and boating around Quartz Mountain.

great state of Oklahoma

Redbud Tree

The state tree of Oklahoma has pink flowers that appear from spring to early summer. Long-tongued bees pollinate the flowers, and many kinds of caterpillars eat its heart-shaped leaves. Native Americans ate the flowers raw or boiled, and also the roasted seeds. In some areas it's called the spicewood tree, because redbud twigs can be used to flavor roasting meat.

Scissor-Tailed Flycatcher

The state bird of Oklahoma is a fantastic flyer. It catches food—grasshoppers, robber flies, and dragonflies—in flight. Males also perform amazing aerial acrobatics while trying to attract females. After finding a mate, they are very aggressive defending their nests, which explains their genus name, *Tyrannus*, or "tyrant-like."

Tulsa

The state's second-largest city, Tulsa was originally settled by Lochapoka and Creek tribes in 1836. They called it "Tallasi," which means "old town" in Creek. Later, it would be nicknamed the "Oil Capital of the World," due to its large number of oil fields. Today Tulsa is home to two world-famous art museums, an opera, and a ballet company.

Underground

Believe it or not, downtown Oklahoma City has a maze of underground tunnels connecting 16 blocks and more than 30 buildings! The first was built in 1931 to connect two hotels. The rest were developed in the '70s and dubbed "the Conncourse," after city leader Jack Conn. In 2006, the Underground was renamed and got a facelift, including new lighting and colors, graphics, art, and photos. Some now consider it a "walk-in work of art."

Vortex

A tornado's vortex is the area in the center of the funnel, the part that whirls around at crazy speeds. Oklahomans know all about it, since the state sits smack-dab in the middle of Tornado Alley. Oklahoma is the third most frequently hit state. Between 1950 and 2009, there were 3,442 tornadoes—that's an average of 53 per year! Yikes!

Will Rogers

Rogers was a world-famous cowboy, stage actor, political commentator, writer, and movie star. Born in 1879 to a Cherokee Nation family in what was then Indian Territory (now Oklahoma), Rogers led an amazing life. He started out in show business as a trick roper in cowboy shows, but went on to make 71 movies and was the top-paid Hollywood star of his time. He wrote more than 4,000 national newspaper columns read by more than 40 million fans. At a time when airplanes were a new invention, he traveled the world many times and was friends with kings, queens, and presidents. It is no surprise that Rogers is known as "Oklahoma's favorite son."

EXtreme Weather

While temperatures in Oklahoma are usually pretty mild, the highest on record is 120°F and the lowest is -31°F. That's pretty extreme! The state also gets its fair share of floods and droughts. Thunderstorms are quite common, occurring 45 to 60 days each year. Add to that giant hailstorms and frequent tornadoes, and you've got one wild-weather state!

Yvonne Chouteau

Chouteau, a Shawnee Indian, is one of the world-famous Five Moons, a group of Native American prima ballerinas from the state. She grew up in Vinita, Oklahoma, and began dancing when she was only four years old! She went on to study at the School of American Ballet in New York, and at age 14 started dancing professionally. Later in life, she cofounded the University of Oklahoma's School of Dance and the Oklahoma City Ballet, bringing her passion for dance to the next generation.

Zoo

The Oklahoma City Zoo, the oldest zoo in the Southwest, started as an accident. In 1902 an endangered white-tailed deer was donated to Wheeler Park, and soon attracted crowds. As more animals were donated, more people came to see them, so the park was officially turned into a zoo in 1903. It's gone through different names and locations since then, but is now ranked one of the top ten zoos in the United States.

Thank you to everyone at the Boys & Girls Club of Oklahoma County for encouraging your kids to write and enter this contest. Thank you to the dedicated Boys & Girls Club staff Jane Sutter and Kristin Minnis, and volunteers Yvonne Maloan and Meredith Williams who guided the youth through this process. Thanks to historian Dr. Bob Blackburn who helped the kids brainstorm topics for the book, and a very special thanks to renowned Oklahoma photographer David Fitzgerald for traveling to every corner of the Sooner State to take great shots for this book. And most of all, thanks to the kids who wrote such fantastic poetry for this book. Way to go!

Photo by Yvonne Maloan

Boys & Girls Club of Oklahoma County is a youth development organization aimed at helping young people achieve academic success, develop good character and citizenship, and live healthy lifestyles. At the Club, youths benefit from a safe, positive environment, supportive relationships with caring adults and peers, a variety of fun programs and activities, opportunities and clear expectations, and recognition that reinforces success. To learn more about the Boys & Girls Club of Oklahoma County, visit our website at www.bgcokc.org.

Rylon Basco

Wneki Borders (H)

Reyna Caldwell (A, P)

Keante' Cooks (Q, S)

Amiya Curry (H, M, X)

Lillian Garaci

Sergio Hernandez (P, V, W)

Saul Hernandez (W, Z)

James Hill

Kalysia Hill

Micyah Hornsby (U, Y)

Tavion Jackson

Tyrone J. Johnson (D, H)

Caroline Maloan (X)

Kianna Marks

Jaylinn Mercado (J, K, L, P)

Kristin Minnis (T)

Caleb Mitchell (A)

Kenneth Mosby

Lyric Nichols (S)

Keely O'Connor (I, R, U)

Ian Perry

Natali Ruiz (P, U)

Jordan Roberts

Mariah Stiggers (E, N, O, U)

Lauren Summers

Jasmine Swindall (A)

Shaniya Tate (F)

Aiden Taylor

Amya Thompson

Zane Tobin

Basil Walker

Asia Williams

Dasia Williams (S)

Mary Kate Williams (G)

Jordan Wood

Michael Young (B, C, H)

Second printing 2016

Library of Congress Cataloging-in-Publication Data
O is for Oklahoma / written by kids for kids.
       pages cm
  ISBN 978-0-88240-911-5 (hardback)
  ISBN 978-0-88240-952-8 (e-book)
  1. Oklahoma—Juvenile literature. 2. Alphabet books—Juvenile literature.
  F694.3.O17 2013
  976.6—dc23

                        2013011044

Published by WestWinds Press®
An imprint of

GRAPHIC ARTS
BOOKS®
P.O. Box 56118
Portland, Oregon 97238-6118
503-254-5591
www.graphicartsbooks.com

Editor: Michelle McCann
Designer: Vicki Knapton

Printed in China

**Part of the growing See-My-State Series,
Written by Kids for Kids!**